Gadget Girl

Story by Carmel Reilly
Illustrations by Wayne Bryant

NELSON
CENGAGE Learning®

Gadget Girl

Text: Carmel Reilly
Series consultant: Annette Smith
Publishing editor: Simone Calderwood
Editor: Jarrah Moore
Project editor: Annabel Smith
Designer: Karen Mayo
Series designers: James Lowe and
 Karen Mayo
Illustrations: Wayne Bryant
Production controller: Erin Dowling

PM Guided Reading
Ruby Level 28

Gadget Girl
Special Effects: Bringing Movies to Life
Banding Together
Play On!
The Power of Wind
Time and Clocks
Amazing Stories of Survival
Wildfire
Southern Skies
Shipwrecked!

Text © 2016 Cengage Learning Australia Pty Limited
Illustrations © 2016 Cengage Learning Australia Pty Limited

ISBN 978 0 17 037305 0

Cengage Learning Australia
Level 7, 80 Dorcas Street
South Melbourne, Victoria Australia 3205
Phone: 1300 790 853

Cengage Learning New Zealand
Unit 4B Rosedale Office Park
331 Rosedale Road, Albany, North Shore NZ 0632
Phone: 0800 449 725

For learning solutions, visit **cengage.com.au**

Printed in China by 1010 Printing International Ltd
1 2 3 4 5 6 7 20 19 18 17 16

Contents

Chapter 1

The Phone Call

The day began like most days. Alexandra James – known as Alex to her family and friends – woke up early. She had a shower, got dressed and sat down to breakfast. The only unusual thing about the day was that her class was going on a field trip to the botanical gardens.

"Now, Alex," said Mum, "make sure you wear your shoes with the auto-adjusting heels. You could be walking up and down hills. And take a self-drying jacket. According to the weather forecast, there might be some showers."

The special clothes came from Gumshoe Gadgets. That was the shop that Alex's family owned. Alex ran up to her room to get the clothes as soon as she finished breakfast.

When Alex came back down, Mum was making sandwiches at the kitchen bench.

Alex looked on in surprise. Making her school lunch was usually Dad's job. Because he was an inventor, he always put interesting fillings in her sandwiches.

Speaking of Dad, why hadn't he been at breakfast this morning? It was oddly quiet without him.

Just then, the phone rang. The call was for Alex's dad. Alex heard her mother say that Dad had gone in early to Gumshoe Gadgets. Alex's mother was quiet for a long time while the other person spoke. Then she said "Yes" and "No" a few times. She sounded tense.

After the phone call, Mum seemed a little distracted. She stared out the window as she pushed the leftover cheese into the bread bin. Then, she slid the bread into the dishwasher and loaded Alex's lunch into her own handbag.

"Mum!" said Alex. "Are you all right?!"

"Goodness me," said Mum, moving everything to the right places. "I was just thinking about what I have to do at work today."

Mum glanced at the kitchen clock. "Oh, look at the time. We'd better hurry or you will be late for school."

Mum worked at Gumshoe Gadgets, too, and it wasn't far from school. She usually took Alex to school on her way to work.

Alex pulled on her shoes, picked up her jacket and backpack and ran out the door after Mum, the heels of her special shoes auto-adjusting with each step.

It wasn't until Mum dropped her off at the school gate that Alex realised she was over half an hour early.

After school, Alex walked to Gumshoe Gadgets to meet Mum and Dad. She couldn't wait to tell them about the trip to the botanical gardens.

She had seen so many amazing plants. Alex had always loved science, and she had learned a lot on the field trip. She was full of suggestions for Dad's next inventions. What about a formula that could turn a seedling into a tree overnight? Or a gadget that could turn any smell into the scent of roses?

"Mum! Dad!" called Alex, as she opened the shop door.

She looked past the shop's display cabinets to the front counter, but no one was there. The door behind, marked "STAFF ONLY", was slightly ajar.

Alex walked through and looked around. There was no sign of Mum or Dad. She was just about to call out again when the door to the cleaning cupboard opened and Mum emerged. She looked surprised to see Alex, as though she had forgotten what time it was. Mum was obviously having trouble reading clocks today.

"What's that terrible smell?" asked Mum, wrinkling her nose and looking around.

Alex checked the bottom of her shoes, in case she'd stepped in something.

"No, no! It's something in there," said Mum, pointing back towards the cleaning cupboard. "I must have left the burner on."

"A burner in a cupboard?" asked Alex, puzzled.

Mum pushed the door open, and Alex leaned around her to peer inside. This cupboard was usually locked, and Alex had never wondered what was inside. She expected it would be boring brooms, buckets and bottles of cleaning liquid. Instead, the door seemed to lead to another room.

Wide-eyed, she followed Mum inside.

Alex could not believe what she was seeing. Not only was this not a cleaning cupboard, it was not any ordinary room either. It was a laboratory. It looked just like the one at school, only bigger and better. Alex could see two long tables, covered with beakers and burners and other scientific equipment. And she could smell a horrible smell, worse than anything you might step in on the footpath. It seemed to come from a pot that was bubbling over a burner on one of the tables.

Mum rushed over and quickly turned it off. She flapped her hand in front of her face for a few moments, before turning on the ceiling fan.

"Phew," she said. "That smell should be gone in a minute."

"Mum," said Alex. "What is this place?" She turned around, looking in amazement at the sophisticated laboratory. "And where is Dad?"

Mum put her hand on her forehead, and took a deep breath. She pointed to a chair close to where Alex was standing.

"Alex, please sit down. There's something I have to tell you."

Alex could feel her heart pounding in her chest.

"What is it?" she asked.

"Your father and I are not exactly who you think we are," said Mum.

Chapter 2

Secrets

Alex stared up at Mum. "So," she said, "who exactly are you?"

Mum sat down in the chair opposite Alex.

"Before you were born," she said, "Dad and I didn't have this shop. We used to work for a large organisation."

"I know that," said Alex, impatiently. "It was a big company in the city."

"No," said Mum. "It wasn't a company. It was NICE."

"Nice? You mean nicer than this shop?"

Mum shook her head. "No, I mean NICE. The National Institute for Counter-Espionage."

Alex's eyes widened. "The government spy agency?" she asked.

"That's the one," said Mum. "I used to be a spy, and Dad made gadgets and special formulas for NICE. We helped to keep the nation safe."

Alex sat open-mouthed. She had never imagined that her parents could have had other, exciting lives like that.

"Wow," she said at last.

Mum continued, "When we decided to leave spy work and start this gadget shop, NICE became one of our top customers. Remember all those orders for Ms Jones?"

Alex nodded.

"Well, Ms Jones is actually Director Jones, the head of NICE."

Alex frowned. "But, Mum, you still haven't told me where Dad is."

"I'm just about to tell you," said Mum.
She glanced around the room. "As you can see, Dad continued to work in his laboratory, making gadgets. Every now and then, NICE asked him to make some formula or other for them as well. Then, two days ago, we got a call from Director Jones. She said that the evil mastermind, Dr Slime, was hatching a plan for world domination. He had developed a formula to turn back time."

"Turn back time!" said Alex.

"Well, not exactly time, but he can turn back a person's age. Drinking his formula would make you younger. While that might sound good to some people, really it would be a disaster. If someone drank too much, they could become a baby! And, as we know, babies are helpless. Dr Slime said that he was going to put enough formula into the water supply to turn everyone into babies – unless the government gave him five billion dollars. Naturally, Director Jones turned to your father to make an antidote, which is –"

"Something that will reverse the effects of the formula," interrupted Alex.

"That's right," said Mum. Then she looked back at the bench and pointed to the liquid on the burner. "Dad was here all last night working on the antidote. But apparently he left here early this morning, and hasn't been seen since. It was Director Jones I spoke to on the phone this morning at home. NICE have been looking for him, but haven't been able to track him down."

She frowned. "It's so unlike him to just leave without telling anyone – and to have his phone turned off. He appears to have gone missing!"

"But you must have some idea of where he went," said Alex, anxiously.

Mum shook her head.

Alex stared into the distance for a minute. "If we can't trace his phone, there is another way we might be able to track him down," she said slowly.

Chapter 3

Keeping Track

"**L**ook at this," said Alex. She and Mum were standing in front of the computer at the front counter. "You know Dad has a special GPS tracker on his watch, don't you?"

"I was so busy thinking about finishing the formula that I forgot all about the GPS tracker," said Mum.

"The tracker is hooked up to our computer system," Alex said, pushing some keys on the keyboard. In a moment, she had the map up on the screen.

"Look, there's Dad's watch!" Alex exclaimed. She pointed to a flashing green dot. "Now we know where it is."

Mum peered at the map on the screen. "That looks like the corner of High Street and Main Street," she said. "He must be at the Elegance Plaza Hotel. Now, why would he go there? And why isn't his phone on?"

"We need to find out," said Alex, quickly plugging her own mobile phone into the computer's USB port and transferring a copy of the GPS tracking app.

"And we need to alert NICE," said Mum. "I'll call Director Jones and we can meet her at the hotel. We'd better take the bike."

"The bike!" Alex squealed, delighted.

The bike was a solar-powered super-scooter. Dad had only recently built it. It was sleek and super fast.

Alex hadn't been for a ride on it yet. She couldn't wait to try it, especially with Mum, who was such an expert rider. Mum liked to race motorcycles in her spare time.

While Mum was making the call, Alex took a few of the gadgets from the shelves. *I might need these,* she thought, quickly tucking them into her backpack.

When Mum returned, she decanted the antidote into a little vial, and put it in her pocket. Then, they pulled on their bike helmets and headed outside.

Mum wheeled the scooter out and started it up.

Alex hopped on the back behind her, and in seconds they were whizzing through the traffic, heading to the city centre.

As they approached the Elegance Plaza Hotel, Alex saw two people in long trench coats walking towards the corner of the street. Mum pointed the scooter in their direction and came to a halt in a parking bay nearby. The two trench coat-wearing people came over.

"This is Director Jones and Agent Swindon," said Mum, pulling off her helmet.

Alex said hello to the two agents. Then she gave Mum's hair a quick pat. "Your hair has gone wild, Mum," she said, leaning close to her ear. Mum's hair looked as though it had lost a fight with a cat.

"Bike helmets!" said Mum, half laughing and half annoyed.

While Mum smoothed down her hair, Alex slipped her phone out of her bag and opened the GPS tracking app. The other three looked over Alex's shoulder. She pointed with her thumb at a green dot flashing on the map. It looked quite close to where they were standing. Alex used the zoom function to pinpoint the signal.

"That's strange," Alex said, after a few seconds. "It looks like the watch isn't inside the hotel at all. It appears to be around here." Alex turned towards an alley beside the hotel.

"Agent Swindon, you go into the hotel and see what's happening," said Director Jones. "We'll search down here."

"I don't like this at all," said Mum, as she strode towards the alley. "There's nothing down here except those big rubbish bins!"

Mum broke into a sprint. Alex was close behind her, glancing at her phone screen as she ran. She could see the green dot growing bigger and bigger. As they came to the first bin, her phone let out a beep.

"You have reached your destination," the phone announced.

Director Jones joined them in the alley just as Mum lunged forward and pushed open the lid of the bin.

Alex stood on tiptoes and peered over Mum's shoulder, her heart racing. She saw a humped shape in the dim light.

"Mum!" she cried. "What is that?"

"Is it …?" Director Jones began, in a hushed voice.

"A bag of rotten potatoes and some cabbage leaves, by the look of it," replied Mum, in a relieved voice.

Chapter 4

Another Direction

"This is always the worst part of this job," said Director Jones. She pulled on a pair of rubber gloves. "Going through the bins."

There were all sorts of things in the bin, from kitchen garbage to the contents of the guest rooms' wastepaper baskets. Alex could see tissues, paper, plastic bags and lolly wrappers among the fruit and vegetable scraps and gooey ice-cream tubs.

Mum pulled out something slimy and covered in carrot tops. "I think I've found it," she said. From her back pocket she whipped out a bottle of spray and a cloth. She wiped at the object until Alex could see that it was Dad's watch.

"Dad must have dumped the watch in the rubbish so that we could find it," said Alex. "I'm sure it will tell us where he's gone."

"Oh, dear, I can't remember his passcode," said Mum.

"I know it," said Alex. She took the watch and punched five numbers into the number pad.

The watch had a recording device. Alex quickly accessed it and pressed the speaker button.

Her father's whispered voice filled the air around them.

"If you are listening to this, you should know that I have been kidnapped. I received a call this morning that I thought was from Director Jones, but it seems it was a call from Slime in disguise. He said to meet here at the Elegance Plaza Hotel.

When I arrived, his henchmen grabbed me. Now they're going to take me to their secret hideout. It's the place where they've been conducting experiments.

I'm in the bathroom of Room 333. I'm going to throw my watch into the bin in the corner of the room now, before they search me. They've already destroyed my phone. I know you'll find my watch later."

Just then, Agent Swindon came racing towards them.

"The people at the hotel said a man answering the description of Dr Slime stayed in Room 333 last night," he said. He looked at Alex's mum. "They saw him leave this morning with another man who looked like your husband, Mrs James."

"I don't suppose Dr Slime left a forwarding address?" asked Director Jones, with a dry laugh.

"No," said Agent Swindon. "The people at the hotel said they got distracted at that point, because a group of children charged through the lobby, all wearing clothes that were far too big for them."

"Oh, dear," said Mum. "It sounds like Dr Slime has been testing the formula."

29

Director Jones had been typing something into her sleek super-phone. Now it started to beep, and she looked up. "I put a number trace on calls to phones in and out of Room 333 last night," she said. "It looks like some of the calls came from a warehouse on the edge of town. It's quite out of the way. I would say it's a perfect place for experiments."

Director Jones gave them the address and, in moments, Alex and Mum were back on the super-scooter, zooming out of town. The two agents followed behind in their car.

It wasn't long before Mum and Alex pulled up near a group of warehouses on the far side of the city. As soon as she got off the scooter, Alex searched in her bag and pulled out a pair of binoculars.

"I brought these X-ray binoculars from the shop!" she said, handing them to Mum.

"Good thinking," said Mum. She focused them on the building.

"Goodness me!" Mum said, after a few seconds.

Mum handed the binoculars back to Alex, who adjusted them for her eyes.

The scene came into focus. She could see into three levels of the building. There were offices and what looked like a laboratory.

The place was full of children, from toddlers to teenagers. Some were carrying boxes, while others were wandering around, looking lost.

Just then, Director Jones and Agent Swindon arrived. Alex handed them the X-ray binoculars.

"It's obvious what we have to do, isn't it?" said Alex. "I'm the only one young enough to go in there and find Dad."

Mum looked worried. "It will be dangerous, Alex."

Director Jones sighed loudly. "I think Alex is right, though," she said. "If our agents storm the place, Slime will release the formula. The best way to do this is to go in secretly. Only Alex can do that."

Chapter 5

The Antidote

The grounds of the warehouse were surrounded by a high wire-mesh fence. There seemed to be just one gate, guarded by two angry-looking teenagers.

How do I get in? wondered Alex, as she studied the fence through the binoculars.

Soon, she found a space at the back that looked as if it was out of sight of the guards and anyone standing at the windows.

"I can snip through the wire with these," she said, producing a pair of sonic pliers from her bag.

"What else do you have in your backpack?" asked Mum.

Alex winked. "A few bits and pieces," she said, pulling on her cap. Then, she raced towards the back of the warehouse.

The operation went smoothly. Alex used the pliers to get through the fence. Once she was through, she used them to mend the wire so that no one would notice. She had just finished when two small boys waddled up to her.

"Who are you?" one of the boys demanded, in a squeaky voice.

"I'm Alex," she said. "I'm checking the fence. And who are you?"

"I'm Jake Miller," said the boy, in an important voice. "I am in charge of security. I don't remember hearing your name before."

"Sorry, Mr Miller, I didn't recognise the 'new' you!" Alex said, with a laugh. "Um … Dr Slime requested that I check this section of the fence. He noticed that no one was guarding this area. Anyway, it's all fine and I'm going straight back to report to the doctor, now."

Jake Miller narrowed his eyes. It was quite a strange expression for a toddler. "All right," he said slowly, as Alex started to stride away.

Alex hurried to the main building. She was confident that she would find Slime there. Surely, he and Alex's dad would be easy to identify among all these children.

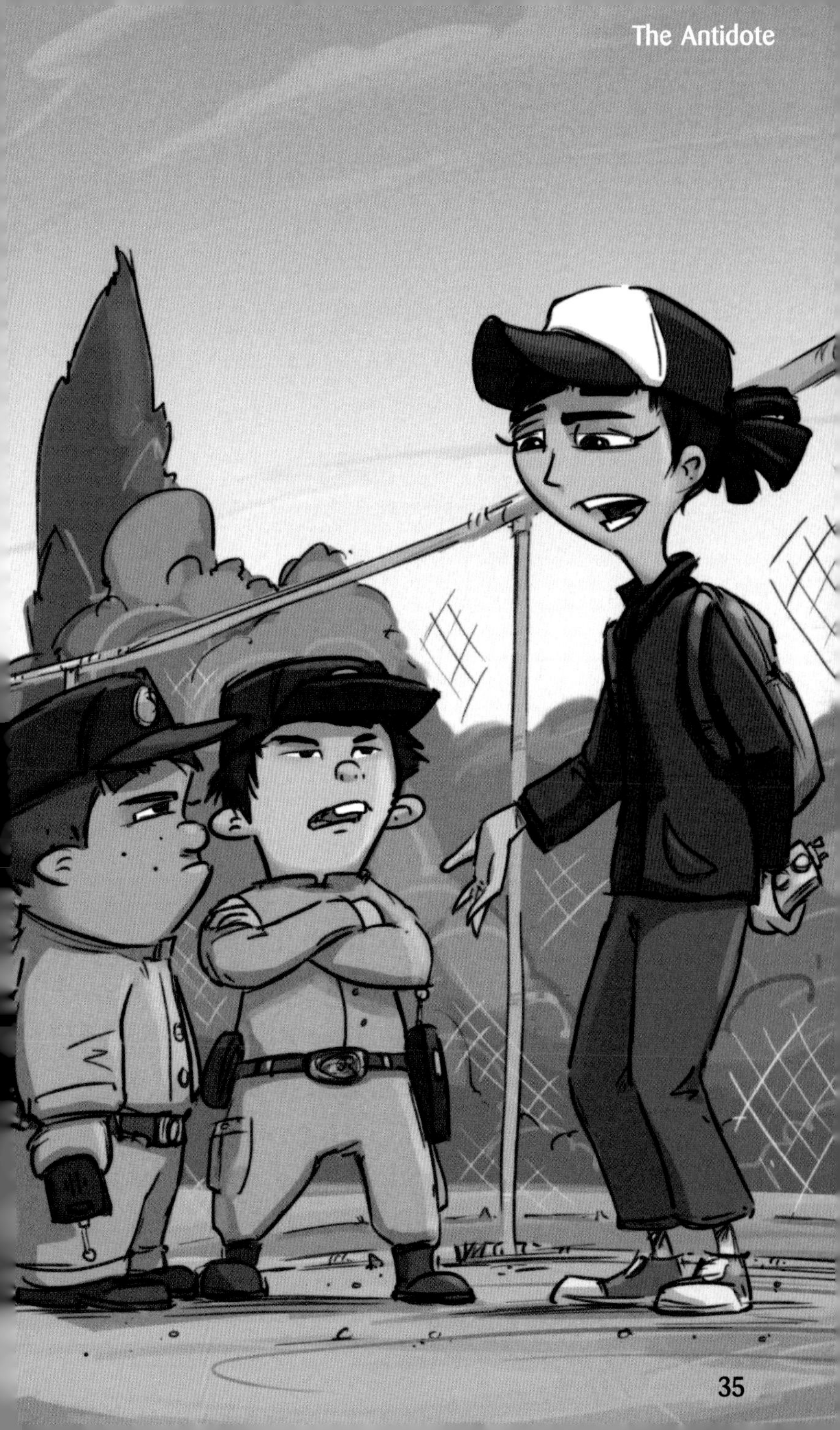

But when she went inside, Alex couldn't see anyone older than thirteen or fourteen. There were children of all shapes and sizes. Babies sat crying, or crawled across the floor. Alex climbed the stairs to the next level, but there still weren't any adults to be seen. Where was Slime? And where was her father? Had Slime done something terrible to him? Alex's heart began to race, and her hands turned clammy.

"Focus, Alex," she whispered to herself.

She walked along a hallway to a large red door, and opened it a crack. This room was the laboratory, and it was full of children and teenagers. Some children were talking, some were playing games and a few appeared to be having an argument. There was no sign of Dr Slime.

Just then, someone tapped Alex's arm. She jumped and had to stifle a scream. She turned around to see a boy of about eight right behind her.

"You gave me a fright!" Alex said, crossly.

"Sorry!" said the boy. He tilted his chin to look up at her, his blue eyes looking deep into hers.

Alex leaned forward. Those blue eyes looked very familiar.

"Alex," he whispered.

She stared at him. "Dad?" she squeaked.

"Shh," said Dad, putting his fingers to his lips. He tugged on Alex's sleeve, quickly pulling her out of the laboratory and into a room off the hallway.

Alex clutched his arm. "What's been going on?"

"Slime brought me here to make a batch of the antidote for him." It was very strange to hear Dad talk in an eight-year-old boy's voice. "I had to use his formula as a base," he continued, "which was lucky. He left me alone for a minute, and I took a drop. When he returned, he couldn't identify me among all of the other kids. I took the antidote with me and sneaked out. Since then, I've been looking around and trying to find out where everything is."

"And?"

"There is a stock of the formula in a room at the back of the lab," Dad said. "We have to destroy it."

"I have a laser," said Alex.

"Excellent, that will be perfect for destroying it all. Just one zap!"

"Let's go in, then," said Alex, grinning.

It was crowded and noisy inside the laboratory. The argument seemed to have escalated, and now almost half the children in the room were yelling at each other.

No one appeared to notice Alex and her dad sneaking through the door and walking casually over to the room at the back.

"There it is," said Dad, as they slipped inside. He pointed to a large plastic barrel.

Alex pulled out the laser. She remembered what it was like to be eight, so she handed it to Dad. "I'm sure you would like to do this," she said.

Dad laughed gleefully as he pointed the beam at the barrel and watched it collapse and bubble into nothing.

"And now it's time to call Director Jones," Alex said, pulling out her phone.

"Oh, no, it's not!" snarled the voice of a young boy.

Alex swivelled around to see a five-year-old with something that looked like a remote control in his hand. The little boy pointed the remote control at Alex, and the phone flew out of her hand and into the air.

"Ha ha!" he screamed.

Dad stepped forward, but the five-year-old pointed the remote control, freezing Dad to the spot.

"This is my all-purpose device," said the child. "It can act like a magnet, or stop people in their tracks, as you can see. How's that for an invention, Dr James?"

"How did you know …?" asked Alex, bewildered. The five-year-old laughed again. "I'm Dr Pertussis Slime, and I know everything," he said. "I took the formula to disguise myself, so that I could fool Dr James into coming out of hiding."

Chapter 6

Too Little, Too Late

Alex stared at the little boy who was really Dr Slime.

"What do you want?" Alex demanded.

"I want the antidote. Now that you have destroyed my formula, I need to make some more. But I have to be my old adult self to make it." Dr Slime held up his tiny child-sized hands. "It's too hard to work with these little fingers."

Dad was still frozen in place, but he could move his mouth to speak.

"I don't know if the antidote will work," he said. "I didn't have time to finish it properly."

"I know about you, Dr James. You just want to prevent me from taking it. Your formulas are always perfect."

Dr Slime rifled through the pocket of Dad's coat until he found the little vial of antidote.

"Whatever you do, don't take it all at once!" cried Dad.

"You think I'm going to leave any for you?" asked Dr Slime, laughing. He opened his mouth and gulped the liquid down.

Alex gasped as she watched the five-year-old change in front of her. First, Dr Slime became a teenager, then a young man, then a middle-aged man. But the formula kept working, until at last Dr Slime was a tiny and very, very old man.

Finally, his frail legs couldn't hold him and he slumped backwards. As he grasped at the door for support, the remote control fell from his hands and clattered to the floor.

Alex leaned forward and scooped it up, along with her phone. She punched in Director Jones's number.

In seconds, she could hear the shouts of the NICE team from outside as they ran into the warehouse.

Mum raced up the stairs as the NICE team were leading Dr Slime away. She rushed past him and hugged Alex. "I can't believe how brave you were," she said.

"She was amazing," piped up Dad.

Mum turned and frowned at him for a moment, before she recognised him.

"Gosh, look at you," she said, laughing. Then she fumbled in her bag and pulled out the other vial of antidote. "Open wide," she said, and squeezed one drop of the antidote onto Dad's tongue.

In a few seconds, Dad had returned to his old self.

"That feels better," he said. He laughed. "Although it was enjoyable to have an eight-year-old's energy for a little while."

Director Jones looked around at the children and teenagers milling about.

"And what about all these other people … er … children?" she asked.

"We can make up enough antidote for all of them, but the formula will wear off after a few days anyway, and people will slowly start returning to their real ages," said Dad. He nodded in the direction the NICE agents had led Dr Slime. "The antidote works the same way. Dr Slime will slowly grow younger, until he's back to his proper age."

"What a shame!" said Mum.

Director Jones turned to Alex and smiled. "Your mother is right. You are very brave. You are also very smart and very good at this sort of work. I might have some missions for you in the future, if you want them."

"I do!" said Alex. She bounced on her toes, excited at the thought of more missions.

Mum frowned. "Only every now and then," she said. "Remember you have to go to school, too."

"I know, Mum," Alex replied, as she removed the back section of Dr Slime's remote control and looked inside. "The invention part of the job is very important, too, so I'll have to work hard at school. I've decided I'm going to take chemistry and physics when I get older."

Dad grinned. "Some things just run in the family, I suppose."

"I suppose they do," said Mum, laughing.